FIVE Little MONKEYS
trick-or-treat

FIVE Little MONKEYS
trick-or-treat

Eileen Christelow

HOUGHTON MIFFLIN HARCOURT

Boston ● New York

For information about permission to reproduce selections from this book,
write to trade.permissions@hmhco.com or to
Permissions, Houghton Mifflin Harcourt Publishing Company,
3 Park Avenue, 19th Floor, New York, New York 10016.

hmhco.com

The illustrations were executed digitally in pen and ink with color.
The text was set in 18-point Cantoria.
Cookie recipe on page 34 courtesy of Tracey Campbell Pearson

The Library of Congress has cataloged the hardcover edition as follows:
Christelow, Eileen.
Five little monkeys trick-or-treat / Eileen Christelow.
p. cm.
Summary: When babysitter Lulu takes the five little monkeys trick-or-treating, they decide to change costumes
with their friends and try to fool Lulu and their mother.
[1. Halloween—Fiction. 2. Costume—Fiction. 3. Monkeys—Fiction. 4. Behavior—Fiction. 5. Babysitters—Fiction.] I. Title.
PZ7.C4523Fk 2013
[E]—dc23
2012025208

ISBN: 978-0-547-85893-7 hardcover
ISBN: 978-0-544-43062-4 board book
ISBN: 978-1-328-86927-2 paperback

Manufactured in China
SCP 10 9 8 7 6 5 4 3 2 1
4500704226

For the latest crop of little monkeys:
Christina, Elin, and Starlin

THE five little monkeys dress up for Halloween.
"Hurry!" says Mama. "Your favorite babysitter is
here to take you trick-or-treating."

Costume
Stuff

3

"Hi, Lulu!" shout the monkeys. "Banana, alien, ghost, goblin, and princess are ready to go!"

"But I was going out with the five little monkeys!" says Lulu. "Where are they?"

"They're taking a nap," giggles the princess.

5

Off they go.

"Ghost, princess, goblin, banana, and alien," Mama reminds Lulu. "Don't lose the rascals!"

"Don't worry!" says Lulu.

Down the street, the alien meets a friend.
"Nice bunny costume!" says the alien.
"I like yours better!" says the friend.
"We could trade," suggests the alien.

"Everyone will be SO confused!" they whisper.

As the other trick-or-treaters run down the street,
Lulu checks: "Banana, ghost, goblin, princess . . .
Uh-oh! WHERE IS THE ALIEN?"

"Here he comes!" exclaims the princess.
"Now, look here, Mr. Alien," Lulu scolds.
"You monkeys need to stick with me!"

"That is the best Halloween trick ever!" whispers the ghost. "I wish I could switch costumes!"
The banana spies two more trick-or-treater friends.

11

It turns out the television would love to switch costumes.
"I'd much rather be a big yellow banana!" she says.

The ghost and the robot switch costumes too.
"This is SO funny!" they squeal. "Lulu will never notice!"

The ghost and the banana catch up just as Lulu is checking again: "Alien, princess, goblin . . . whew! Ghost, banana!"

"Everyone is switching costumes!"
giggles the goblin. "This is so silly!"
"We could switch costumes too!"
suggest two more trick-or-treater friends.

15

"Good idea!" says the goblin. "This is the best Halloween trick!"
"Pleased to help," says the pumpkin.

The grapes and the princess decide to trade too.
"Lulu won't even notice!" says the princess.

When the goblin and the princess catch up,
Lulu doesn't SEEM to notice a thing.
"You monkeys are just in time!" she tells them.

Then Lulu counts, "Princess,
goblin, ghost, alien, banana . . .
Oh, good. I have all five little monkeys!"

The other trick-or-treaters think THAT is hilarious!

But then Lulu hustles the princess, banana, goblin, ghost, and alien down the street.

"See you around!" she calls to the other trick-or-treaters. "We have to get home for a big Halloween treat!"

"Uh-oh!" cries the big blue bunny.

23

Lulu delivers the banana, ghost, alien,
princess, and goblin home to Mama.
"I didn't lose one!" she says.

Mama gasps. "They look different!"
"Oh, don't worry about THAT!" says Lulu.
And then the doorbell rings . . .

"Trick-or-treat, Mama!"
Mama looks very carefully at the trick-or-treaters.

"There must be some mistake," she says. "Because I am the mama of a banana, alien, ghost, princess, and goblin. And they are already home."

Mama closes the door . . . almost.

"Uh-oh!"

But then she peeks out.

"Why don't you rascals come in for a treat?"

29

Mama hugs her monkeys, then scolds them. "Poor Lulu! This is trick-OR-treat, not trick-AND-treat!"

"That's okay," says Lulu. "I've made the perfect treat for tricksters!"

"Eyeballs and worm juice!"

33

LULU'S EYEBALL COOKIE RECIPE
(Borrowed from her aunt Tizzie)

3½ cups all-purpose flour

½ teaspoon salt

1 cup unsalted butter (softened)

⅔ cup sugar

1 egg

1 tablespoon corn syrup

1 tablespoon vanilla

Mix the flour and salt together in a bowl and set aside.

Cream the butter and sugar in a large bowl.

Stir the egg, corn syrup, and vanilla into the butter-and-sugar mixture.

Add the flour-and-salt mixture, one-third at a time, until the dough is mixed.

Wrap the dough in plastic wrap and chill for an hour or two (or even several days). When ready to shape into eyeballs*, let the chilled dough warm until it is soft enough to work with.

Preheat oven to 350°F.
Bake the cookies for 6 to 10 minutes. Check at 6 minutes. You don't want them to get too brown!
Let the cookies cool, then frost them with white chocolate (see recipe on opposite page).

*Note: This dough can be shaped into all sorts of Halloween creatures. It's like working with clay...but it's edible!

IF YOU DON'T HAVE TIME TO BAKE, DOUGHNUT HOLES OR ROUND VANILLA COOKIES MAKE GOOD EYEBALLS!

WHITE CHOCOLATE FROSTING

1. Melt a bag of white chocolate chips in a microwave or double boiler. Stir until smooth.

2. Dip baked and cooled cookies in the melted white chocolate. Place them on a wax-paper-lined baking sheet.

3. Color the remaining melted white chocolate blue or green with food coloring (for irises). If you want brown eyes, melt some semi-sweet chocolate.

4. After letting the white chocolate harden, dip the baked eyeball cookies into the colored chocolate to create iris-size circles.

5. Use chocolate chips or melted semi-sweet chocolate for the pupils of the eyes.

WORM JUICE

Use limeade or lemonade concentrate mixed with water or seltzer. Add a handful of gummy worms.

OR

Mix your own limeade or lemonade, using a cup of freshly squeezed juice to approximately 2 quarts of water (or seltzer) and adding sugar in small amounts until you get the taste you want. Add a handful of gummy worms.